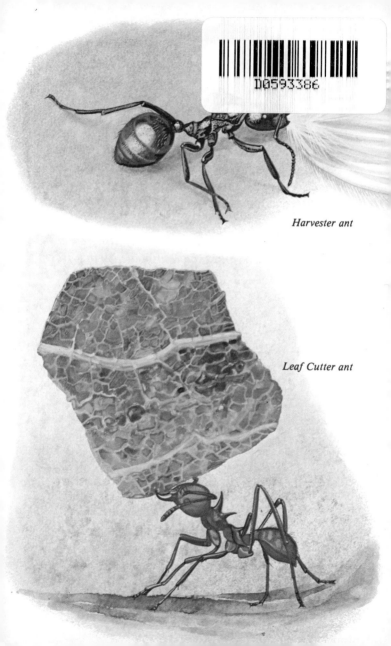

Harvester ant

Leaf Cutter ant

Finding ants is never a problem. Ants find us. In the spring and summer they seem to be everywhere. If you sit on a grassy area eating a strawberry jam sandwich, you will soon attract unwanted company. Foraging ants will scent the sticky crumbs, eat their fill, lay a trail for others to follow, and return to their home under a nearby rock. Soon hordes of hungry, eager and busy little black creatures swarm all over you, the sandwich, and anything else that is edible.

Ants are fascinating as well as irritating creatures. They are very complex small animals, living in highly organised societies, leading the most extraordinary lives.

Acknowledgments

The author and publishers wish to acknowledge the assistance of Mrs Dorothy Paull in the preparation of this book. They also wish to thank the following for photographs used: page 51, Ardea London (H & A Beste, K W Fink); page 10, Jane Burton/Bruce Coleman Ltd; pages 21, 39, 40/41, Stephen Dalton, Natural History Photographic Agency; cover and pages 6, 43, 47, Natural History Photographic Agency; pages 5, 11, 12, 13, 16, 19, M M Whitehead.

© LADYBIRD BOOKS LTD MCMLXXX

The story of the
Ant

by JOHN PAULL
illustrated by IAN FRY

Ladybird Books Loughborough

Insects and ants

Insects have existed on our planet for millions and millions of years, long before even the dinosaurs. An ant is an insect, which means it has six legs, and three sections to its body: the head, the thorax and the abdomen. Like bees and wasps, ants are members of the order of insects called the *Hymenoptera*.

Ants are similar to man in that they are fitted to live in nearly all environments. They inhabit almost every part of the world except the very cold regions like the Polar Zones. Wherever small land creatures exist, ants are sure to be found. Ants never live alone however as most insects do. They are social animals, living together in large groups. Hundreds of thousands live in large, complex nests under stones and paths, under grass, in dead tree trunks and old buildings – and some even in kitchens. Some ant species make vast underground nests with narrow, dark connecting tunnels and carefully constructed chambers for storing food and keeping the ant eggs snug and safe, spacious areas for larval rearing, and even cemeteries for dead ants. These nests stretch for metres beneath the earth. Another kind of ant, the large brown wood ant, piles up dead tree leaves, pine needles and twigs, and weaves them all together to make a big mound or fortress, which may be as high as two metres above the ground. Hidden away is an intricate system of galleries and chambers. Similar ant hills are a feature of the rugged North Wales landscape. The soil and grit that is piled high by the ants is then colonised by feathery moss, and tricks many a weary walker who sits down for a rest.

Each ant has a special job to do in the nest. Some care for the eggs, tend the young, and look after the cleaning, whilst others go searching for food.

Wood ant hill

Lasius niger – Black ants

Recognising ants

Everybody knows what ants look like. The ant that is seen most often in Britain is black and called Lasius niger, which appropriately means the black ant. Lasius niger nests under stones and slabs in the garden. If you pick one up very carefully and look at it under a magnifying glass, you will see that what gives an ant its unique look is its pinched waist, just between its abdomen and thorax. It has a large head in proportion to the rest of its body, powerful jaws that are called *mandibles,* well suited for the purpose of biting and carrying food, and two long, bent feelers *(antennae)*, attached to the top of the head.

The antennae

The antennae are the ant's main sense organs. As many of the ants in a colony have very bad eyesight (some are even totally blind), they rely on picking up scent trails with their feelers to find their way from place to place. When they discover food some distance away from the nest, ants lay a trail to the newly-found food supply, and the other ants follow with their antennae close to the ground, and make their way home on the same path.

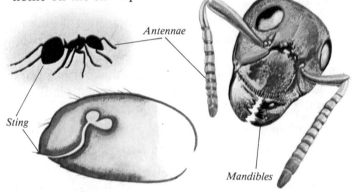

Antennae

Sting

Mandibles

The ant sting

In Great Britain, most types of ants kill their prey by attacking in such large numbers, biting furiously with their mandibles, that they eventually succeed in overpowering the victim. Then they tear it to pieces which they carry back to the nest. The Wood Ant, however, is different. It has a sting that paralyses its prey with a poisonous liquid called *formic acid*. The sting does not penetrate the victim. The acid is sprayed through the sting, covering the caterpillar or worm, making it motionless.

queen ant

Ant types

In every ant colony you can find at least three types of ants living together in harmony, each kind depending on the other two for survival. As with all insects, there are male and female ants, but unlike other insect groups, there are two different kinds of females. They are the queens and the workers.

The queen

The queen ant is the most important ant in the whole colony, as you would imagine from the regal name. She is the biggest ant, and normally lives in the centre of the nest where it is warm and safe from danger. The other ants build a special chamber for the queen, and fuss over her, giving her the best food, and tending her every need. The queen builds new colonies and all through her life lays thousands and thousands of ant eggs, year after year, keeping the huge ant family thriving. She lives for about fifteen years. If all the ant queens in a colony die through disease, the other ants soon become very agitated and appear to forget their work routines. Before long, the entire colony ceases to function properly and perishes.

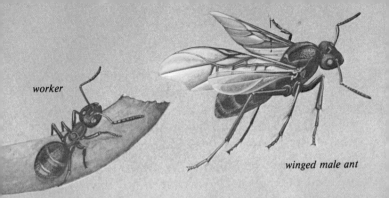

worker

winged male ant

The workers

Worker ants are female and rarely lay eggs. They are smaller than the queen and one would expect to find thousands of them in a single colony. Industrious and energetic, worker ants are well named because they do all the hard ant work. They care for the queen, prepare her chamber, feed her with special food and wash her, pandering to her in a non-stop buzz of activity. They rear the young and carry them to safety when danger threatens from marauding wasps or other fierce creatures. Workers search for food and collect enough to feed everybody else in the nest. Many of them are nest sentries and guards, fighting off invaders. They soon wear themselves out and only live for about two years.

The male ants

The males have wings and are cared for by the workers. They do not have any special jobs in the nest. When the time comes, they leave the nest in vast swarms with the young queens, mating in flight with queens from other nests, helping to produce new generations of ants.

The life cycle of an ant – I

An ant, like other insects, goes through a series of complicated body changes throughout its life, from egg to adult ant. This process is called *metamorphosis,* which means that each stage in an insect's life looks quite different from the previous one.

The life cycle begins when the queen receives the sperm of the male ant. (This sperm can stay alive in her for several years.)

Young black ant queens

She scoops out a hole and lays her first batch of eggs. Eventually they develop into helpless larvae with very small heads and no legs. They are cared for and fed by the queen until they pupate and change into adult worker ants which immediately take over the duties of ant rearing. Now the queen lays more eggs, fertilising some with the sperm and not others. The real work of the nest begins.

eggs in egg chamber

larvae

pupae

The life cycle of an ant – II

The eggs change into larvae and are cared for and fed by the new workers. As they are unable to look after themselves the feeding is forcible, the workers *regurgitating* (that is, bringing back food they have themselves already swallowed) the food directly into the mouths of the larvae. When the larvae are fully grown, they spin oval cocoons around themselves, and the next stage of metamorphosis begins. Very slowly the developing ants *pupate* (grow into their adult forms) inside the cocoons. The so-called 'ant eggs' that are sold in petshops as goldfish food are in fact these cocoons.

At last the pupa develops into the familiar ant, and kicks at the inside of the cocoon. At this sign, the worker tending it bites through the hard covering, and the new adult ant crawls out, taking its place in the ant society. The adults are males, workers or queens, depending on whether the eggs were fertilised or not, and on the amount of care, attention and food that has been lavished upon them during the development. The males come from unfertilised eggs, and those ants that are the new queens would have been given the very best food when they were larvae.

The final stage in the cycle has now been reached. The workers begin their new life, working for the good of the others. The males eat and rest until they are ready to mate with the queens from other nests, and the new queens gather strength before they leave the nest to begin another colony.

winged males

The nuptial flight

During hot, sticky summer days, thousands of winged males take to the air in pursuit of airborne young queens from different nests. This is called the *nuptial* or *marriage* flight.

Several nests can erupt into frenzied flying movements at the same time, filling the air with clouds of black swarming dots. Swallows, housemartins and sparrows are just three examples of birds who swoop and devour the defenceless ants in their thousands.

Fortunately, some of the male ants successfully meet and pair with the queens from other nests, and fertilise them with sperm. The males that survive the nuptial flight and avoid being eaten by birds are not welcome back in the parent nest, and are pushed away by worker ants. They soon die from exhaustion, exposure and lack of food.

However, the fertilised queen flies further away from her parent nest, and searches for a suitable place to lay her eggs.

When she has found one, the queen lands and quickly scoops a tiny hole in the ground. She lays a small number of eggs in it, then lies on them to keep them warm and safe.

As she has no further use for her wings, she rubs them against the soil until they fall off. The wing muscles inside the thorax provide her with food to last throughout the following winter. The queen stays wrapped round the eggs until the next spring.

15

tunnels in ant nest

Inside an ant's home

When spring comes the eggs change into larvae, which then spin cocoons, and eventually emerge as adult workers. These small, underfed worker-daughters now take charge. Their first job is to tend the ailing queen, who is tired and weak from her winter work. They tunnel up through the ground and go in search of something nutritious. When the queen is fed and refreshed, she lays more eggs, and the workers begin to extend the nest by building numerous tunnels and chambers.

As the nest grows, new batches of eggs are removed to special chambers by the workers. Here the eggs are regularly turned by the nursing worker ants who lick and feed on the oily substance that covers the egg shells. This daily licking makes the shells sticky and the shells stick together, giving them warmth and protection. In hot weather after rain, the ants place the larvae in large groups, sorted according to size, a few centimetres beneath the soil surface. This makes sure the larvae get enough warmth and moisture. The new eggs develop into bigger adults than the first generation, because they have been given more and better food by the workers collecting food from the surrounding countryside.

The nest increases in size as the workers co-operate to build more chambers with connecting tunnels. They create rooms for food storage, egg resting, larvae rearing, and even chambers for ants to die inside the nest. The queen's own chambers increase in size and comfort, giving the queen space to rest and to lay more and more eggs. She is not the only egg layer in the community. Occasionally the workers produce unfertilised eggs which develop into males. All the eggs are removed each day and placed in the resting chambers, and the queen is cleaned and fed regularly. The ant nest becomes a vast underground labyrinth of tunnels, chambers and galleries measuring several metres in length, filled with industrious ants.

When winter comes, the activity inside the nest slows down. During really cold spells the ant colony goes into a state of hibernation.

Ant food

Take your eyes from a cream cake at a picnic for just a moment, and it will be covered by nibbling ants. Ants cannot resist sweet things, even though they eat many kinds of tiny animals and plants. The sweetest food they find in the wild is honey and nectar that they collect from plants and small creatures.

Like other insects, ants are always searching for food outside the nest. They sometimes go quite a distance away, laying a chemical trail so that they can find their way home. When they come across something edible, they eat as much as they can before returning to the ant colony. Not all of the food is digested, however. They carry much of it in their crop, the part of their body that acts as a stomach. Other worker ants meet them in the nest tunnels, stroking the returning foragers with their antennae, making them regurgitate much of the food collected. The food collects in small puddles on the floor of the tunnels. This is eaten by the others, and some of it, in turn, regurgitated to the queen and the developing larvae in the larval chambers. More worker ants then leave the nest, follow the trail laid by the successful group, and the process is repeated.

Even though many kinds of ants are *omnivorous* (eating both plants and animals), some are *carnivorous,* only eating flesh, and others are *herbivorous,* preferring plants. The British wood ant is a carnivore, having a special liking for small creatures such as caterpillars and small worms. The wood ants hunt in packs, attacking and stinging their prey then

ripping it into small pieces with sharp teeth. Pieces of
the victim are carried back to the nest in the ant's
mandibles and in the crop, to share with the hundreds
in the colony. Well-established wood ant colonies
clear quite large areas completely of small creatures,
so they need to roam some distance away from their
home in a constant search for food.

Wood ants attacking moth

The clever ant

Ants are clever insects. *Entomologists,* people who study insects and the way they live, consider ants to be the most organised and seemingly intelligent of small creatures. So marvellous is the way ants live together, so clever seem their methods of building homes and getting their food, that some eighteenth century observers thought they were able to reason and work things out in their heads. But, unlike man, ants cannot reason or learn. Even so, their life pattern is highly complex. The way ants carry out their particular jobs in the ant colony never varies. A single ant never does anything out of the ordinary, and does not display any individuality like humans. Ants have developed through millions of years an ingenious, unalterable, inbuilt programme which helps them to survive in the wild environment.

Life in the vast underground ant nest is set to a series of unbroken routines, each ant having a job to do that contributes to the success of the whole colony. Some jobs are complicated, some easy. The male ants do nothing except mate with the queens, whilst the workers perform all kinds of difficult tasks. Workers construct intricate and beautiful nests to provide a home for perhaps as many as 50,000 ants. Building an ant nest is a co-operative group activity. The workers help each other to build all the necessary chambers and tunnels, linking the food storage chambers with the larval rearing rooms, so that an abundant supply of food is always available for the fast-growing young ants. As they work, the worker ants appear to talk by

Wood ants 'talking' to each other, antennae touching

stroking each other with their sensitive bent antennae, passing on important information through the nest to other workers. They use the same method for identifying creatures they meet in the underground tunnels or on the ant paths on the soil.

21

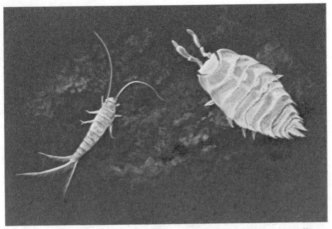
Bristletail and White Woodlouse

Ant guests

Ant colonies are huge. As many as 50,000 ants live together quite happily underground, moving in and round the tunnels and chambers, going about their daily routines. In many ways, ant colonies are like our cities, with living accommodation, food stores and interconnecting roads. In our homes we often have enough space to put up our friends and relatives. Ants, too, like guests. If we were able to take off the top of an ant nest like a lid and look inside, hundreds of creatures other than ants would be seen scuttling from the light. Many are there as guests because the ants need them, and others because they have chosen to live among the ants. Scientists have counted over 1500 different living things making their homes in ant nests.

There are caterpillars, tiny beetles, white woodlice, mites, scale insects, bristletails, greenfly and blackfly.

aphids and honeydew

Greenfly

Many ants feed entirely on the sugar secretions of other insects, especially greenfly and blackfly. Greenfly and blackfly belong to a group of insects called aphids. Aphids normally live on the sap of plants. They are common in our gardens, appearing as clusters on the sides of our plants, busily sucking the life-giving sap. Plant sap contains a high amount of sugar-low protein, and the aphids suck as much as they can from the plants for their needs. Because they take so much, the excess sugar is excreted (passes out of their bodies) by the greenfly and blackfly in the form of honeydew. This can often be seen in gardens and meadows as liquid bubbles sticking to the stems of flowers and grasses. The bubbles are drops of strong sugar in solution.

Milking greenfly

Ants search for the greenfly and blackfly and bring them back to the ant nest. Carefully the workers stroke the aphids until they are stimulated to excrete the honeydew in small droplets. Immediately the honeydew appears, the worker ants drink it, storing some in their crop for the larvae and for the queen ant who lies in her special chamber producing more and more eggs, but unable to collect food for herself. Some ants collect aphids' eggs and take them back to their home, placing them in the larvae rearing chambers. They are looked after until they hatch into aphids, and then

taken to nearby plants where they suck the sap. As they produce honeydew they are stroked by the ants, who gorge themselves on the sweet-tasting substance. The herds of greenfly are kept close to the nest and protected by the ants from marauding ladybirds and other predators who feast on aphids. Lasius niger, the common black ant, collects greenfly that feed on the shoots of plants. Different types of greenfly suck the roots of grasses, and the yellow ants that live near the roots of grasses collect root-sucking aphids in their underground nests.

milking greenfly.

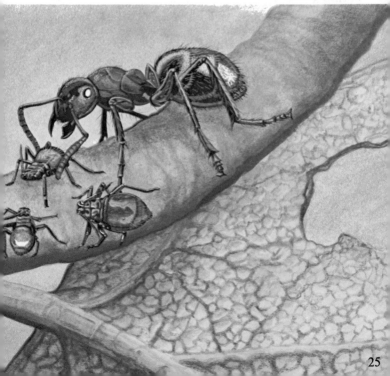

Caterpillar guests

Ants are attracted to caterpillars of many species of Blue butterflies because they produce a liquid similar to honeydew. The caterpillars of the Chalk Hill Blue (Lysandra coridon) are collected by workers from yellow ant colonies and kept underground. The Large Blue (Maculinea arion) lays its eggs on a plant called wild thyme that grows close to ant nests. When the eggs hatch into caterpillars they are rounded up by workers and taken underground to chambers deep in the nest. Here they are tended and milked like aphids for their honeydew. The caterpillars stay alive by eating ant larvae. When each caterpillar eventually pupates and changes into the adult butterfly, it crawls

larva of Large Blue butterfly

Large Blue butterfly

through the dark tunnels to the daylight and then flies away. It soon finds a mate, lays eggs on the wild thyme, and the life cycle begins again.

Beetles

Some beetles and mites also live as guests of the ants. As they spend all of their life underground with the ants, they are totally blind, finding their way round by using their senses. They would be quite helpless without the companionship and help of the worker ants. Another creature found living deep in the ants colony is the blind white woodlouse. The woodlice, the beetles and the mites help the ant because they are scavengers, eating the debris the ants leave in the tunnels and chambers that would otherwise rot. They clean up the nest thoroughly, stopping the spread of unwanted mould.

Blind Beetle and Springtail

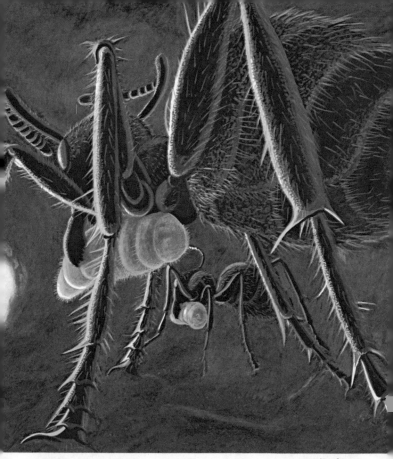

ant carrying larva

Ant slaves

Some ant colonies thrive on slave labour. The daily busy activities that go on deep inside their nest, like rubbish clearing, building, caring for the young, and food collecting, are all done by slave worker ants.

Raiding parties of worker ants scour the countryside in search of other ant families. They force their way past the guard ants, break into the larval chambers, and carry the larvae away in their mandibles, fighting off the worker ants as they go.

The larvae are placed in special larval chambers, and, after a long period of time, eventually pupate, changing into fully developed workers. These ants spend the rest of their lives doing all the hard work for their captors. Escape is out of the question because they think they belong to the captors' colony, having changed from larvae to adults in the slave owners' chambers.

Some ants do not have any workers at all, depending entirely on slave labour. The queen of one particular slave-making ant, which is found all over Europe, has an exciting and daring way of starting her colony. She enters the nest of a rather timid ant and steals the pupae. She guards these very carefully until they become workers able to look after her offspring. Later, the ants raised by the slaves will raid other nests of timid ants and bring in more slaves.

Some communities would die without the slaves, because the slave owners do not know how to collect food or look after their own young.

The queen of the shiny black ant in Great Britain enters the nest of the yellow meadow ant and settles down. The yellow ants look after her eggs as carefully as they tend their own. After a time, yellow ants and black ants are seen in the nest together. What happens to the yellow ant queen is a mystery, but after a while her workers die out and the colony only contains black ants.

Ant enemies

Occasionally hunting spiders will break into a colony of ants, killing and eating as many as they can before being chased away by soldiers and guards. Centipedes enjoy eating ants but would not think of entering the nest and fighting a few thousand workers.

Man is the main enemy of the ant. Even though ants do us no harm in the garden, unless they nest in the middle of the vegetable plot and cause the roots to die, man kills ants by the thousand. As ant workers collect and share their food with other ants in the

ants attacking a marauding spider

digging up an ant hill

colony, whole nests can be destroyed by adding poison to the sweet food they love so much. Commercial ant killers work on this principle. The worker swallows infected food, takes it back to the nest, regurgitates it, and thus spreads the poison throughout the nest.

All this seems unnecessary, as the ant is the gardeners' friend. As they tunnel from their nest to the air, they aerate our soil. They kill thousands of soil pests for food. Scientists have estimated that a mature ant colony in a garden will eat up to 50,000 insects a day.

Keeping ants – I

It is not wise to keep any small creature in captivity without thinking about what it involves beforehand. We have to bear in mind that the creature's natural habitat has to be understood and reconstructed as much like the original as possible, otherwise the life of the captive insect will be unpleasant and perhaps painful. Remember, we enjoy comfortable homes, good food at frequent intervals throughout the day, and the freedom to come and go as we please. We must attempt to do the same for any living thing we keep for observation purposes.

Good homes for small creatures can be easily made after careful planning, and we can learn a great deal by observing the animal's routine.

Making an ant farm

Worker ants will not form a new colony without the queen. It seems only the queen can begin a new nest and produce the first brood of workers who take over the task of extending the home. Therefore, if you want to keep ants for a short period of time to observe their habits, first find your queen.

Look carefully under garden slabs and rockery stones that are being moved in the garden by the gardener in your house, and you will probably spot lots of black ants scuttling round with eggs in their mandibles. These are the workers carrying the eggs to a safe place. Search for the queen, collect her in a matchbox with some workers, and introduce her to her new home.

workers carrying eggs

Keeping ants – II

The illustration shows an ideal way to keep ants because it allows freedom of movement for the ants and gives you the opportunity to watch them make a new home. Remember ants need protein, so give them a little meat to eat.

The hollows in the corners can be used for placing small quantities of jam or meat for the ants to collect. If you drill a small hole as shown in the picture, and leave the box outside in the garden, the workers will come and go as though it were a natural home.

Teachers sometimes need ants to study in the classroom. A laboratory home can be made from two pieces of perspex and a framework of wood. The framework is filled with a mixture of light soil and sand, as in the diagram. Food and water can be given through the plastic tubing.

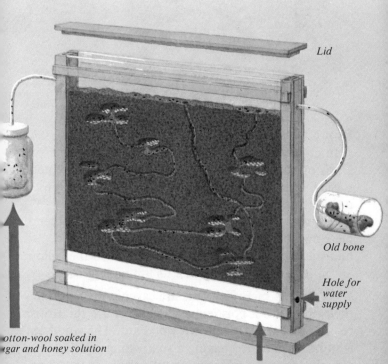

Lid

Old bone

Hole for water supply

otton-wool soaked in gar and honey solution

Plaster of Paris

Exotic ants

Wood ant stinging

In Great Britain there are about forty different kinds of ants, the most common being the black ant, Lasius niger. This is closely followed by the yellow meadow ant which is not often seen as it lives underground between the roots of grasses. Another meadow ant, Lasius flavus, lives in orchards and undisturbed grassy places, but is similar to the yellow ant in its habits, spending all its life underground.

Two kinds of British ants are carnivorous and kill their prey with a poisonous sting. They are the British red ant and the large brown wood ant. The wood ant is quite formidable, having a sharp sting which contains formic acid, a powerful poison. If you turn over a wood ants' nest out in the countryside, the workers will swarm all over your hands. Biting hard with their mandibles, the ants will bring up their hindquarters between their legs and squirt acid into the little wounds they have made with their teeth. Neither the bite nor the sting will hurt for very long, but the attack would easily kill a small creature like a butterfly.

Pharaoh's ant

The smallest ant in the world also lives in Great Britain but not in the wild countryside or under our garden lawns. Pharaoh's ant prefers the warmth and comfort of kitchens and larders. It is about 2 mm long and lives in small colonies. Once established in a kitchen, it is very difficult to get rid of, feeding off the crumbs and other morsels we leave behind after we finish our meals.

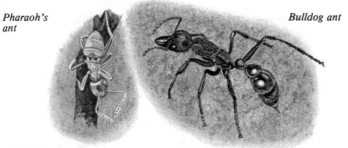

Pharaoh's ant

Bulldog ant

Bulldog ant

In contrast to the Pharaoh's ant, the biggest ant in the world is the Bulldog ant that lives in the deserts of Australia. The Bulldog ant has a sting over 2 cm long and huge vicious jaws that rip prey into small pieces. It can leap several centimetres in the air when it attacks other creatures, stinging them with a very strong poison that even hurts man.

Parasol ants

The parasol or leaf-cutting ants are perhaps the most remarkable ants in the world, leading the most interesting and complicated lives. Living in tropical South America, the parasol ant colony numbers thousands of individuals. There are several different kinds of workers in the nest, some with enormous heads and mandibles, and some quite small. The small workers scour the countryside in large numbers, foraging for tree leaves, stripping trees bare.

The leaves are cut into pieces that the ants carry back to their nest in their mandibles. The pieces are quite large and as the ants walk along the trail to the colony it looks as if they are carrying umbrellas, hence the name, parasol ants.

The small workers take the leaf pieces to the large-headed workers, who set about cutting them into smaller sections with their sharp teeth. The leaves are then chewed and taken deep in the nest where there is a thriving toadstool garden. The damp, chewed leaves are placed on top of the small toadstools, and they, too, soon support a luxurious growth of fungi.

The ants love the fine threadlike *hyphae* (roots) of the fungi, and crop it daily for their larvae, queen, males and themselves. The ants' excreta is put on the garden each day by workers and this keeps the toadstools flourishing.

This particular fungus has been cultivated by the ants for millions of years, and is seldom found growing wild.

When young queens leave the parent parasol ant nest, they take fungal spores (seeds) with them from the garden. So when they create their own nest they can make their own toadstool garden, by collecting the leaves, chewing them and adding the toadstool spores. When the first brood of workers develop they take over the care of the garden and the collection of new leaves. As the nest matures and more workers are in the community, the garden gets bigger and bigger to support the ant population. Other kinds of leaf-cutting ants make toadstool gardens out of rotten wood, seeds, and animal dung.

Leaf Cutter **ants**

Army or driver ants

No ants are more feared than the army or driver ants of Africa. As well as being the most fearsome of the ants, they are also different from other ants because they are nomadic, which means they do not have a fixed home but move from place to place.

The incredible thing about them is that all army ants are totally blind, relying on their antennae to give them all the information other creatures get from their eyes.

Army ants hunt in large columns of millions of individuals, each following the other by using scent trails. They are as savage as piranhas, the flesh-eating fish. Even the largest and fiercest animals are helpless before them, and are driven frantic by the millions of bites unless they can flee to the safety of water to drown their tormentors.

They are carnivorous, and life is a perpetual search for food. As they group together in such large numbers, whole areas are quickly denuded of small creatures. All kinds of living things are eaten by the voracious ants. Even large animals locked by man in cages or pens are killed by the hungry swarms and devoured in a few hours.

In the centre of the marching columns is the huge queen. She has a body swollen to such a size that walking is difficult, so she is carried by the worker ants. They are flanked by the males, and surrounded by hordes of soldier ants with great jaws and a formidable sting. On the outside of the column are scouts, scenting the presence of food.

Army ants on the march

The march of the army ants is periodically halted and they rest in hollow tree trunks. It is then that the queen lays more eggs, which are carried by the workers when the march resumes. One South American species occasionally makes a nest by huddling together to form a snug home. When the young develop, the whole colony moves on until the queen is ready to lay eggs again.

Honeypot ants

Honeypot ants

In America, Australia and Africa, the hot, dry season limits the growth of plants and cuts down the amount of sap available for creatures like aphids to suck. Honeypot ants only collect honeydew from aphids during the wet season, having an ingenious way of storing the sugar solution and saving it for the times when the food is not readily available. The honeydew is carried back to the underground nest in the ants' crops and fed to workers who spend their entire lives hanging from the top of ant chambers like swollen storage caskets. These storage ants get bigger and bigger as more and more food is forcibly fed into their bodies. They get so fat they are unable to move.

When the workers want to feed from them they are stroked and they regurgitate the honeydew. Sometimes they get so big they burst, creating a rush of activity as the ants swarm over the dead storage ant licking up the spilled liquid.

Weaver ants

Weaver ants are found in hot countries like Australia and Africa. They are agile climbers, and actually spend most of their lives high up in trees. They build their nests from tree leaves they secure together in an odd but clever way. The leaves are pulled together and sewn with silk from the weaver ants' cocoons. The strange thing is that the sewing is done by worker ants holding live cocoons in their mouths and threading them through punctured holes in the leaves, at the same time unravelling the silk. This keeps the leaves together, forming a warm, secure nest for hundreds of the weavers.

Weaver ants sewing up leaf

Harvester ants

Harvester ants, particularly the type which lives in North America, are the most well known plant-eating ants. The harvester workers collect different kinds of seeds from a variety of plants and store them in underground chambers made by other workers. When the ants are hungry, the workers break open the hard outer husks of the seeds with their tough mandibles to get at the succulent seed contents. The workers digest what they require, and regurgitate the remainder for their queen and young. Occasionally, the store of seeds gets so large that the warmth and moistness of the chambers makes them go soft. When this happens the workers take them outside in the daylight and leave the seeds to harden again in the sun.

Harvester ants

Carpenter ants (found only in North America)

Carpenter ants

Carpenter ants are large, black insects that make
their nest in newly dead trees, nibbling away at the
decaying bark, making space for the colony. As the
colony gets bigger and bigger, the whole tree becomes
a complete network of tunnels and galleries, with
workers, males and the dominant queen carrying on
their daily routines. Carpenter ants are timid and
forage for food at night. Armed with sabre-like teeth,
they can destroy buildings by tunnelling into the
wood.

45

Termites or white ants

White ants are more properly called termites. They are different from true ants and are rarely white in colour. Nevertheless, they are similar in their life style to ants and are well worth getting to know.

Termites are only found in warm climates, and are common in the continents of Australia and Africa. They live in a variety of dwelling places.

Some termites inhabit rotten tree trunks and nibble away at the soft wood, making passages that link up the separate chambers and rooms they need for their queen and their young. These primitive termites number not many more than a thousand individuals in each colony.

In contrast to these, more advanced termites build huge solid structures called termitaria that are as high as ten metres above the ground. As a rule, termitaria do not occur in considerable numbers in a restricted area, but there are exceptions to this.

In Cape York in Australia, there is one of the most remarkable termite cities in the whole world. Over two square kilometres of land is covered with pointed pillars about three metres high, each housing about 200,000 termites. The termitaria are made from wood fibre chewed by the termites into pellets that are used as mini bricks. Inside each of these towering structures, the worker termites build a complicated system of arches and tunnels, strong enough to support the massive weight of millions of wood fibre pellets and millions of active termites.

In Africa the largest termites of all live in huge termitaria that house as many as 2,000,000 termites, living in close proximity to one another in friendship and harmony.

a termitarium

The termite family

The members of each termite colony all come from a single pair, the king and queen termites. They mate and produce workers, soldiers, and winged male and female termites that leave the nest as a swarm to mate with termites from another termitarium.

The worker

The termite worker is blind. Its job is to look after the eggs and the developing young termites, and carry out most of the industrial work of the community. Workers clean up the termite refuse, shift the dead bodies to termite cemeteries, and build new tunnels and chambers, continually extending the termitaria. The termite workers outnumber all other termites in the colony, and they live for about two years.

The soldier

The soldier termite has an enormous head and very large mandibles. It is blind and wingless, spending all its life in the termitarium, blocking gaps through which invaders could crawl, and frightening attackers by noisy movements of its head and thorax.

Winged termites

The winged male and female termites prepare throughout the year for the summer swarming when they mate with termites from other homes. They are cared for by the workers and fed with large quantities of food to prepare them for the nuptial flight. When they are airborne they fall prey to birds and some large flying beetles. Man also enjoys eating termites, and in some parts of Africa they are a delicacy.

King and queen

Each termite colony has one king and queen, (unlike the ants). They are the royal pair, living in a royal cell, and looked after by hordes of workers who cater for their needs.

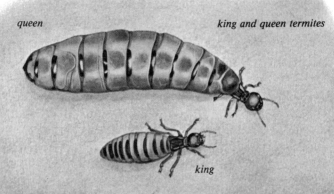

queen

king and queen termites

king

Termite food

Like the parasol ants, the largest species of termite (it lives in Africa in huge termitaria) feeds entirely on a small fungus it produces underground. Spores of the fungus are deposited by workers on specially prepared wood fibre that has been chewed and laid flat in a gardening chamber. The spores mature into small toadstools that are tended and cropped by the workers. Termites do not like the toadstool stalks, but prefer the *mycelium*, which is a mass of fine root-like hairs that the toadstool grows in the wood fibre.

Year after year in the termitarium, the gardens prosper, getting bigger and bigger, keeping step with the growing numbers of termites in the colony. The huge garden chambers are ideal for the growing of toadstools because the atmosphere is warm and moist.

The ant-eater

Termites and true ants in tropical countries have a menacing predator: the great ant-eater, sometimes called the ant bear. The ant-eater is one of the most curious looking animals in the world. It has a long head and a snout which looks like a rubber tube, and it does not have any teeth. It measures about two metres in length from head to tail.

Grey in colour, the ant-eater has a broad black band on its chest. It lives in the depths of hot, steamy, humid forests and swamps, feeding on termites and ants. The ant-eater's powerful claws rip down large sections of the termitarium, and as the termites rush to repair the damage, the ant-eater's